EBOXCAR
Warner, Gertrude Chandler,1890
Sam makes trouble /

071907

WITHDRAWN

# Sam Makes Trouble

CREATED BY

## Gertrude Chandler Warner

ILLUSTRATED BY

## Kay Life

Albert Whitman & Company

Morton Grove, Illinois

You will also want to read:
**Meet the Boxcar Children**
**A Present for Grandfather**
**Benny's New Friend**
**The Magic Show Mystery**
**Benny Goes into Business**
**Watch Runs Away**
**The Secret under the Tree**
**Benny's Saturday Surprise**

Library of Congress Cataloging-in-Publication Data
Warner, Gertrude Chandler, 1890-1979
Sam makes trouble / created by Gertrude Chandler Warner;
illustrated by Kay Life.
p. cm. — (The Adventures of Benny & Watch; #9)
Summary: When Benny's friend comes to visit the Alden house with his
two-year-old brother Sam, the younger boy makes trouble everywhere he goes.
ISBN 0-8075-0646-X (pbk.)
[1. Behavior — Fiction.] I. Life, Kay, ill. II. Title.
PZ7.W244 Sam 2002
[Fic] — dc21
2001005711

# The Boxcar Children

Henry, Jessie, Violet, and Benny Alden are orphans. They are supposed to live with their grandfather, but they have heard that he is mean.

So the children run away and live in an old red boxcar. They find a dog, and Benny names him Watch.

When Grandfather finds them, the children see that he is not mean at all. They happily go to live with him. And, as a surprise, Grandfather brings the boxcar along!

One day, Benny's friend Tyler came to play. His little brother, Sam, came, too.

Sam was only two years old.

"Thanks for watching the boys," Tyler and Sam's mom told Grandfather. "I'll be back soon."

"Don't worry," said Grandfather. "Everything will be fine."

"You'd better keep an eye on Sam," Tyler said. "He's trouble."

"He doesn't look so bad to me," said Benny.

Grandfather gave the boys some cereal for a snack.

Sam grabbed the cereal box. The cereal spilled all over the floor.

"Sam!" Tyler said. "You made a mess!"

"Don't worry," said Benny. "We can clean it up."

Benny and Tyler cleaned up the cereal. Watch helped, too.

"Come on, Sam," Grandfather said. "Let's go for a walk."
"No!" Sam shouted. "Play with Benny!"

"It's OK," Benny said. "I'll play with him."

"I'll be right here," Grandfather said.

"Let's do a puzzle," Benny said.

The boys got a big puzzle. It was hard to put the right pieces together.

"Go toilet," Sam told his brother.

"I'll go with him," Tyler said.

Sam and Tyler went to the bathroom. Then Benny heard Tyler shout, "Sam, no!"

Benny ran to the bathroom.
Tyler was looking in the toilet.
There was a piece of the puzzle
in the toilet!

"All wet," Sam said.
"Yuck!" said Benny.

"I'll read Sam a story," said Benny.

Benny got a book about trucks. He read it to Sam.

"Sam like trucks!" said Sam.

Then Benny and Tyler read some more books. Sam looked at the pictures.

It was nice and quiet. Watch
took a nap. So did Grandfather.
Tyler looked kind of tired.
Benny felt a little sleepy, too.

Suddenly Benny looked up.
Sam was gone!

"Where's Sam?" Benny asked
Tyler.

"Not here!" said Tyler. "Uh-oh.
This is trouble!"

Grandfather woke up. "I'll look outside," he said.

"I'll look upstairs," Tyler said.

"I'll check downstairs," said Benny.

Benny looked in the kitchen.
No Sam.

Benny looked in the living room.
Sam wasn't there.

Sam wasn't in the dining room, either.

Suddenly Benny heard Watch barking. "Watch," Benny called. "Where are you?"

Watch barked again. Now Benny knew where he was!

Benny ran to the bathroom. Watch was sniffing under the door. He looked at Benny.

"Sam," Benny called. "Are you in there?"

"I go toilet," Sam called.

Benny turned the knob. It didn't move. The door was locked!

He could hear the water running. "Sam!" Benny shouted. "Open the door!"

"I wash hands," said Sam.

Benny called, "Tyler! Grandfather! I found Sam!"

Tyler and Grandfather came running.

"He's locked in," said Benny.

"Oh, man!" said Tyler. "I *told* you he was trouble!"

Benny peeked in the keyhole.
Sam was standing on a little stool.
He was squeezing toothpaste all
over the sink.

"I brush teeth," said Sam.

"Do you have a key?" Benny asked Grandfather.

"The key is lost," Grandfather said. "You have to unlock the door from inside."

"Let's break it down," Tyler said. "I'm pretty strong."

Benny had an idea. "Maybe the bathroom window is open."

"Good thinking," Grandfather said. "Tyler, you stay here and talk to Sam. We'll go outside and check the window."

Grandfather and Benny went outside. The window *was* open.

Grandfather called inside, "Sam, can you open the door?"

"I flush toilet," said Sam.

He flushed the toilet. Then he flushed the toilet again.

Benny said, "If you can push up the window, I can climb in."

"Are you sure?" asked Grandfather.

"I'm sure," said Benny. "I am an excellent climber."

Grandfather pushed up the window.

Benny got a box. He climbed on the box.

Grandfather helped a little. Watch barked.

Then Benny climbed through the window!

"Hi, Benny!" said Sam.

Benny turned off the water.
He took Sam's hand.
He unlocked the door.
"You *are* trouble," he said.

Tyler was waiting outside the bathroom.

"Hi, Tyler!" said Sam. "Sam hungry!"

Tyler was mad. "I'm going to tell Mom, Sam," he said. "You are bad news!"

Sam looked sad. "Sam sorry," he said. A tear rolled down his cheek.

Then Benny had another idea. "Grandfather, ice cream would make everyone feel better."

"Sounds good!" said Grandfather.

Tyler smiled a little. "I *am* kind of hungry," he said.

"Sam like ice cream!" said Sam.